HOUSEHOLD WORMS

Household Worms

Stanley Donwood

This preview edition published 2011
by Nosuch Library, Bristol, England.

ISBN 978-1-906-47755-4

A CIP catalogue record for this book is available from the British Library.
Stanley Donwood has asserted his right under the Copyright, Designs and
Patents Act of 1988 to be identified as the author of this work.

Typeset in Baskerville by Ambrose Blimfield
Decorations by Zachariah Twain
Giro cheque cashed by Otto Wilkinson
The cover shows a detail of 'Fleet Street Apocalypse' by Stanley Donwood
Print management by Jon Lewis EPM

www.slowlydownward.com

NOSUCH LIBRARY is an imprint of Tangent Books,
Unit 5.16 Paintworks, Arnos Vale, Bristol, BS4 3EH
TEL. 0117 972 0645

WWW.TANGENTBOOKS.CO.UK

FOR M+I+K

Contents

Wage packet

DURING A PERIOD of poverty more pronounced than usual I consider applying for a job. A concerned friend suggests that I try for a place at the restaurant where she was, until recently, employed as a waitress. The most usual position to come up is that of a dishwasher. My friend warns me that dishwashers are considered the lowest of the low, an underpaid subclass treated abominably. She tells me that in a restaurant there is a structured hierarchy of abuse; the owner harangues the manager, who insults the chef, who turns angrily on the preparation staff, who vent spleen on the waiting staff, who then unleash their fury on the dishwasher. The dishwasher has very little room for manoeuvre in this concatenation of spite. I assure my friend that I will be fine, and ask her for directions to the restaurant. The chances are that I will not need the job, that something will turn up.

A week later my financial situation has not improved, so I take a bath, put on some relatively clean clothes and walk to the restaurant. The manager cannot see me as he is 'off sick', but after a lengthy wait I am summoned to the office, where the assistant manager introduces herself to me. The office is small, and smells of things which I cannot identify. She asks me why I want the job. I say I had always wanted a career in catering. She asks me if I have any experience, and I reply that I am keen to learn. She wants to know if I work well as a team member, whether I am what she refers to as a 'people person' and also whether I have any prior convictions. After a passing reference to the conduct expected of her employees, she outlines my responsibilities and the hours I will be required to work.

I ask her if that means I have got the job, and she answers that she will be in touch. I leave the restaurant with mixed feelings. On the one hand, I think I dealt with the interview quite well. However, I failed to get the last job I applied for, and that was only to work as a shelf stacker - or rather, a 'replenishment operative' at a downmarket superstore near the ring road. But essentially I feel positive about my prospects.

Three days later I receive a telephone call from the assistant manager. She enquires about the possibility of my working in the kitchens that evening. I ask her if that means I have got the job, and she answers that we will have to see how things go. This evening's work will be both a 'trial period' and a 'training session'. I want to know if I will be paid for the work, and she tells me that 'training periods' are not paid. In fact, she adds, with something of a giggle in her voice, perhaps I should pay for this training. I laugh sycophantically and put the phone down. The sky outside begins to rain, and I look around my room, as if for the last time.

The restaurant is very busy. There is a queue outside, and the waiters and waitresses look harassed. I am hustled through the dining area to the kitchen, which I see houses two red-faced, angry chefs, three furious prep staff, and two large unattended sinks piled high with dirty dishes and pans.

My 'training session' involves a great deal of washing up. The clientele of this particular restaurant seem to make a lot of mess, and appear to delight in stubbing cigarettes out in their unwanted burgers, fried eggs, prawn cocktails and pork chops. I am also introduced to The Pig, which isn't a pig but rather a large metal machine. The Pig is kept in the very back room of the restaurant, along with large empty metal tins that once contained cooking

oil and empty cardboard boxes. I pour food
scraps scraped from plates into a bucket, which
I then tip sloppily into one end of The Pig. I
press a green button, and The Pig shakes and
emits a terrible noise made of crushing bones
and churning matter. When the noise subsides
and the food scraps are all gone I press a red
button, and The Pig shudders to a halt. Then I
return to the sinks and try to catch up with the
piles of crockery that have accumulated during
my time away.

By the end of the evening I am very tired,
but the assistant manager calls me aside, and
she insists that I join her and some of the waiters
for what turns out to be four hours of lager and
a great many cigarettes. We all agree that
the catering business is a tough business that
attracts people who are the 'salt of the earth'. I
feel very agreeable when I finally get home, and
I fall asleep easily, dreaming only of detergent
and the sound The Pig makes as it digests the
leftovers.

In the morning I feel considerably less
sanguine. When I remember that I agreed
last night to a shift at the restaurant starting at
one o'clock I groan loudly and slump back into
my bed. I realise that I worked for six hours

and have nothing except a headache. Outside the sky is raining again and the seagulls are mocking me.

At around half past one I walk through the dining area to the room at the back. The assistant manager looks very cross, and tells me that she will be docking my wages because of my lateness. She asks me if I have 'punctuality issues'. I say that I have not, and ask her how she can dock wages that I don't have. This is the wrong thing to say.

Later, when I am called upon to clean out the pork buckets, I realise my headache has subsided. The job in hand is, however, so thoroughly nauseating and dispiriting that I take advantage of a lull in the restaurant's activity to step outside for some fresh air. The assistant manager joins me and offers me a cigarette. She begins to tell me that she isn't really a bitch and when she was a little girl she wanted to be a ballerina. Because the fucking manager is 'off sick' she has to do all the fucking work and really she wants a quiet life in a cottage in the country. It would be different if she was the manager. For a start she would be able to afford a better car and a better house. I sympathise, and then decide to take advantage of her mood and ask about my wages. She glares furiously at me, asserts that I drank them last night, had the temerity to turn up late on the busiest day of the week, and adds that the only reason she hasn't sacked me already is because she is a good person and is determined to give me a chance.

During this interlude both of the sinks have filled with plates and cutlery, and wearily I begin to empty one sink so I can fill it with water and detergent. After scraping the plates free of unwanted food and greasy cigarette butts I take the now full bucket to The Pig. I press the green button, and feed The Pig with something approaching tenderness. Soon I will be forced to share its diet. I can see myself squirrelling choice leftovers into my pockets to be devoured later, out of sight of the rest of the staff.

Eventually the last customers leave the restaurant, meaty arms draped around one another. My chores keep me busy for another half an hour, and when I hang up my apron and head for the door I am stopped by the assistant manager and invited to share a table with her and three waiters, one of the chefs and two of the food preparation staff. I protest, saying that

I cannot afford to spend any more of my wages on lager. They look confused, until the assistant manager says something quietly to them, whereupon they burst out laughing. It seems that the assistant manager was only joking with me about that particular matter. The lager is a perk of the job, a fringe benefit. It occurs to me that to have a fringe you ideally need a main event, such as a wage, for the benefit to be attached to. However, I am too tired to mention it, and drink lager for several hours. The assistant manager may have wanted to be a ballerina, but the chef had always dreamt of a career in the army, two of the waiters were actually 'resting' between acting jobs, the third intended to be a comedian, and the food preppers both intended to become property developers.

The night ends in raucous laughter, toasts to the 'salt of the earth' (ourselves) and jokes about how ill we will all feel in the morning. I stumble home through the rain, thinking generous thoughts about my co-workers, and eventually fall into a sleep filled with dreams about the glutinous matter that stubbornly adheres to the bottom of the pork buckets.

I am awoken from my gritty sofa by an infuriated hammering on the front door. It is my landlord, who has a determination to collect the last two weeks' rent. I clutch at my temples and tell him about my new job. This seems to assuage his incipient fury, as long as I pay him as soon as I get my wages, and he leaves, muttering dark threats about bailiffs. This morning, I realise, will not be productive. I trudge up to bed, anxious to sleep the remaining hours until my one o'clock shift begins.

I make pains to arrive on time, and the assistant manager nods curtly at me as I don my apron. I know for certain that I am extremely hungry, but the leftovers I scrape into the bucket repel me, coated as they are in cold, coagulated grease and studded with crushed cigarette butts. I ask the chef who wanted to join the army if I can have a burger. He flips one over and passes it to me on a metal spatula, warning me that it will 'have to come out of my wages'. I am not sure if he is joking or not, and he turns his red face back to the griddle before I can ask him.

The burger is still pink and raw at its core, but I eat it rapidly, feeling a surge of energy almost immediately. I redouble my vigour with the dishes and pans, and before long the bucket is full of waste food. I go to feed The Pig, and it gurgles as I feed it. I have saved the leftover desserts for last, and The Pig lets out a contented belching sound as I pour in melted Knickerbocker Glories. But then there is a terrible sound of grinding, a shrieking, shearing noise that fills me with alarm. Hastily I press the red button, and The Pig judders on the concrete floor before falling silent. For a minute or two I stand still, the empty bucket in one hand, the other hand hovering a few inches away from The Pig.

When I tell the chef who wanted to join the army what has happened he too stands motionless for a short time. Then he turns to face me, shaking his head, and says that I'd better go and tell the manager. I remind him that the manager is 'off sick'. He says that I had better tell the assistant manager, then. Still shaking his head, he returns to the griddle. With trepidation I leave the kitchens and wait in the busy dining area until the assistant manager notices me. She walks rapidly towards me, flicking her finger to remind me of my grease smeared clothing and generally unkempt appearance, and she mouths unfriendly words. The force of her personality pushes me back through the door into the kitchen, where she stands very close to me and asks me what exactly do I mean by barging into the dining area like that. I explain the dreadful noise that The Pig made, and she marches through to the back room with me scurrying at her heels. She presses the green button, and again The Pig makes that hideous screaming noise. The assistant manager presses the red button and turns to me, her eyes narrow slits, her face red, her whole body shaking slightly. I find it difficult to imagine that this woman could ever have dreamt of tutus and ballet pumps. I picture her in them, and release an involuntary smile with my mouth. This is the wrong thing to do. The screaming that comes from the assistant manager is even worse than that which came from The Pig, which was at least non-verbal. She calls me a great many names, implies that my brain is retarded and that I am impotent, that my penis is smaller than her little finger. It seems that I have inadvertently fed The Pig a piece of cutlery. This will do terrible things to the grinders, she says. She tells me that because she is only the fucking assistant manager she cannot sanction calling in the fucking mechanic. I ask if we can't telephone the manager and ask him to sanction it, but she spits furiously at me that he. Is. Off. Sick. And then she tells me I now have to empty the buckets of scraps into the empty cooking oil cans, and she storms off, to get back to some real work and away from fucking imbeciles such as myself. Oh, and the damage to The Pig, when it has been costed, will come out of my wages. This is bad. The empty oil cans are quite large, but after three shifts here I know how much waste is fed to The Pig. There are only about twenty of the oil cans in the room, and I calculate that they will be full after the end of this evening. But there is nothing I can do. I am in disgrace in the kitchen. Nobody speaks to me, and I tend to the sinks, washing dishes, drying cutlery and so on until the prepping staff wordlessly push the pork buckets across the floor to me. On my trips to the back room The Pig sits idle while I pour the slops into the cooking oil cans. The room begins to smell quite abominable, and I worry that the ghastly odour of the intermingled food waste will drift through the dining area, getting me into even more trouble. I wedge open the top window, hoping that the smell will be drawn out into the night air. After work I am not invited to drink lager with the others, and make my way home disconsolately through the rain. I have no food at home, and nothing to drink except tap water. I sit for a while looking out of the window, and then suddenly I have an idea.

The rain has stopped, and although it is still very windy the sky is clearing, and stars are visible through the orange haze of the city. In the alley which the restaurant backs onto I see that the top window of the back room is still wedged open, as I left it. I find a crate and stand on it, reaching through to unlatch the larger part of the window. Once inside, I close the window and turn on the light. Any hopes I might have had of salvaging something to eat from the oil cans are immediately quashed by the foul state of the mess within them. Then I realise – of course! The kitchen is full of food. I can help myself! Once in the kitchen I help myself to several prawn cocktails, a salad and some of the burger buns. I look longingly at the frozen burgers and decide to try to turn the griddle on. I place several frozen burgers on the bars, figuring that what I cannot eat now I can take home with me.

Suddenly I feel quite full, and sit outstretched on the floor. Then I begin to feel guilty. If the assistant manager finds out about this I will be quite done for. Not only will I get the sack without even having got paid, I will actually owe money for breaking The Pig. By now the food must be sustaining my mental faculties, for I have another brainwave.

In the back room I find a spanner, and study The Pig. It looks as if I can remove the side plate, which should reveal the inner workings. I am not of a mechanical bent, but I reason that it should be relatively easy to locate the errant piece of cutlery and extricate it somehow from the grinders. So I kneel to undo the bolts on the side panel and work it free from its housing. And then, in a gusting rush, a tide of revolting slop shoots out of The Pig, drenching me and spreading rapidly in a noisome flood all over the floor. The stench is atrocious, and without being able to stop myself I vomit copiously again and again, desperately crawling backwards through the filth on my hands and knees away from the still flowing river of macerated burgers, egg, bread, prawns, cigarette butts, pork and various accompanying dishes.

I reach the wall opposite and haul myself into a standing position. I am now dry retching, and my first meal in some time is mingling with the lake of effluent at my feet. As I try frantically to work out what to do, I hear a roar from the kitchen. The griddle! I wade through the disgusting goo to the kitchen door and push it open, inadvertently allowing the backed-up sludge to pour through. To my horror the entire griddle area under the extraction hood seems to be on fire, my burgers barely visible through the flames as charred lumps on the bars. Without hesitating I splash back and grab the bucket, scooping up about half a gallon of slop from the floor, and rush back into the kitchen to fling it at the griddle. To my relief the flames die back a little, so I repeat the exercise several times more until the fire is completely out. I stand there, the empty bucket dangling from my hand, surveying the full horror of the situation. I have never seen anything even remotely as disgusting as the scene before me.

I tell myself that this is impossible. How can a long-handled teaspoon from a Knickerbocker Glory glass have caused this devastation? The kitchen and back room are flooded with the foulest liquid imaginable, the griddle and the walls adjacent to it are splattered and flecked with the same, the griddle itself is probably beyond repair, and I myself am covered almost head to toe in mashed, rotting leftovers and my own vomit. The smell is horrendous, and I cannot help but notice that the flood is seeping into the dining area under the swing doors that separate it from the kitchen. And, of course, The Pig is still broken.

I cannot stand it. I am incapable of anything except escape. I leave, slamming the back door behind me. The wind has stopped, and with every step the stench wafts up to my nostrils. Eventually I get home, and with incredible relief turn on the shower, peel off my sodden clothes and stuff them into the bin. I stand under the shower for what could be hours, then dry myself and fall into bed, and then into sleep.

In the morning it takes a while for the gravity of my predicament to sink in. I cannot decide what to do, and the fact that I am afflicted with a ravenous hunger does not make clear thought any easier. At last I decide to turn up for work at one o'clock as normal, and feign complete ignorance of what has happened.

When I arrive I am considerably disconcerted to find the premises cordoned off with Police incident tape. The staff are huddled outside, talking urgently and I walk over, and innocently enquire about what has happened. The waiter who intends to become a comedian tells me that the restaurant is now a murder scene. He says that the early shift arrived to find the place in complete disarray, that there had been a fire and something like a burst sewer pipe had flooded the ground floor. It had been the sanitising contractors who had raised the alarm when they found what they thought were human finger bones in the sewage. The Police had arrived, and sealed the building with blue and white tape. No-one was allowed in.

Overcome with conflicting emotions I walk a short distance away and sit down on the pavement. Human finger bones? It is all rather too much. After the trauma of the previous night I cannot take this new development in. I have to eat something. I walk back over to my colleagues and broach the subject of our wages, and what is likely to happen now that there will be no work at this establishment for some time, or, more likely, ever. The other chef, the one who's aspirations I am unaware of, tells me that there is little chance of getting paid now. No-one has been able to contact the manager, and in any case it is doubtful, even if he were to arrive, that the Police would allow access to the safe.

I'm not feeling very good. I leave, and then remember my friend, the one who recommended that I get a job at this restaurant. I walk over to her house, and she lets me in, looking very concerned and asking if I'm all right. I answer that I'm not, not really, and recount my awful experiences since I last saw her. And I ask her if she has any food.

After eating a sandwich and drinking a brandy I'm beginning to feel a little clearer. My friend has heard about the restaurant murder on the radio, which is why she was looking so worried when I arrived. That, and the fact that I looked terrible. I ask her if she thinks that I will be a suspect, because I must have left fingerprints all over the place last night. She doesn't think so; she tells me that all the staff will have done the same. And in any case, she says that the radio said that the Police are treating the disappearance of the restaurant's manager as 'suspicious'. Apparently he first went 'off sick' when she was still working there, and no-one has seen him since that time. I ask for another sandwich.

We listen to the radio, but apart from what the Chief Superintendent calls 'significant developments' and an 'ongoing investigation' nothing much has happened. The corpse has been partly reassembled and 'is thought to be a male in his mid-to-late forties', which my friend tells me fits the description of the manager. I think of The Pig, and those bone crunching sounds it made. I had almost come to feel affection for it, but now my feelings are more of revulsion. The fact that I have been sprayed with the decomposed and macerated remains of the manager makes me feel quite horrible. We get the brandy out again and I'm afraid that I drink most of it.

At six we turn on the television set to watch the news, but I am a little too drunk to focus on it properly. I fall into a doze, but my friend wakes me by shaking my shoulder. The television screen swims into view, and I watch with shock as I see the assistant manager, screaming in a most familiar way, being manhandled into the back of a Police van, lashing out and spitting at the Police. The reporter announces that she has been arrested on suspicion of murder, then tells the viewers how it is alleged that she dismembered the manager and fed him to The Pig, which the reporter refers to as a 'waste disposal unit'. It further transpires that she has been raiding his bank accounts to make a deposit on a rural property and to invest in a prestigious ballet academy.

I am astounded. It isn't that I like the assistant manager, but it is the fact that she had confided in me, told me that she had once dreamt of being a ballerina, and of living in the country that bothers me. I feel almost like an accomplice, especially when I think of The Pig. I think I am in some sort of shock. I fall asleep again.

When I awaken it is the morning, and my friend has gone to work. She has left me a note, saying that I can stay there and to help myself to anything in the kitchen. I trudge desultorily to the refrigerator and drink some milk. I realise with a dreadful empty feeling that I still have no money. There is a local paper in the sitting room, and I sit on the sofa, leafing through the 'situations vacant' pages, imagining what appalling horror will befall me when I next try to earn a wage.

Straw

I'VE GOT THIS job now and there's a lot of travelling involved. Mostly I'm in London, out in the suburbs, the places out at the ends of the tube line. Ever been to Harrow or Wealdstone? Amersham?

Anyway, the upshot is that I don't get home really, except at weekends. I was staying with friends to start with, but the manager says, oh get a grip for fuck's sake. Then he says, what you doing, kipping on fucking sofas? Fucking state of you. Suit all rumpled to fuck and smelling of dog. Stay in a fucking B&B why don't you. Charge it. Expenses isn't it? Fuck sake. Then he just shrugs at me and goes back into his office. He needs to relax.

I don't mind sleeping on sofas, but maybe he's right about the smell of pets. It can't be good for business. So I start booking into these bed and breakfast places, and some of them, well, I'd rather be on the sofa smelling of dog. But still, I'm not going to argue. And all of this is fine really, absolutely fine. Then I have this horrible day when I am on my way out to somewhere near Romford and I see this traffic accident and the bloke who gets knocked over, you can tell he's copped it straight away. Poor bastard never stood a chance. I don't hang around like some of those ghouls, waiting for the ambulance and the cops and that. I'm off on my way, but I tell you, it shakes me up badly.

Two days later and I'm north of Bromley and this old dear keels over outside McDonalds and would you believe it? She's only died, hasn't she? This time I reckon I've got to wait for the emergency services. But it turns out I'm not required. I tell the driver what happened but he's busy and just nods and tells me to be on my way.

Coincidence, I tell myself, but the next day there's another fatality when my job takes me down to Epsom. It happens again in Romford, and again three days later up at Waltham Abbey. I start getting really bothered after another two, and over the weekend I can't sleep properly for worrying that I'm cursed or something. I tell my mates about it at the pub on Saturday night and they just take the piss. I laugh too.

On Monday night I'm staying in this B&B up Hendon way. There's one bloke there, staying in one of the upstairs rooms, and everyone knows he's really ill. I'm sweating a bit, thinking, oh no, not again, please. I go to bed, none too happy, and when I'm at breakfast the first thing I do is say, that bloke upstairs, he okay is he? Turns out he's fine - well, not fine as such but not dead. I'm really relieved, and I say goodbye after I'm done and head out, thinking to myself, thank fuck for that.

I'm fifty yards down the street when I realise I've forgotten my bag, so I pop back to pick it up. I'm on the hallway, just about to leave for the second time when I hear this voice saying, help. It's the ill bloke, and I knock on his door saying, you okay? No, he says, so I go in to see what he wants. He's only in the act of dying, and he wants to hold my hand while he goes. I take his chilly hand and hold it and look despairingly at the door, thinking, this is the last fucking straw.

In it, out of it, in it

Walk up a long ago road covered with moss
Into the woods
There's snow forecast
I want to lose myself in a blizzard
No snow here though
Just distant traffic and birds speaking
     to one another
Sit on a dead tree
Grey sky

Grey feathers spread across the moss
A beak: bloody flesh still attached
Red against pale green
A siren, far off

All around the crows shout about me
Snagged by brambles
Whipped by thorns
I dread other humans
Tiny flakes fall
Cold dead skin

Push through spiny undergrowth
A muddy plateau.   Frozen ruts
The sound of traffic and aeroplanes
Hard to think
Leaning against barbed wire
Two flocks of birds, above the bypass

An unattended fire dying
A circle of hot grey ash
A bird dips then plummets
A cold east wind
Into the woods.   A snowy path
Walk into an abandoned quarry
Caves everywhere
Warm air that smells of blood drifts out
And I'm too scared to go very far in

I lose my way
Emerge blinking from the woods
A golf course
I'm hungry
I wish it would snow
A dark pubic thicket in the crotch of a beech
A ruined house
A sign; private woods no access
Branches glow in the sunlight

Look out at the sky from the top of this hill
I think I'm surrounded by blizzards
One swoops over
Walk into it, the sun still out
My shadow clear as summer
Snow down my neck
Watching valleys full of snow blow towards me
No shelter; eyes watering from the cold wind
Snow faster and faster, tapping on my coat
Falling fast
Hypnotic
I'm becoming a snow man
Hands too cold almost

Sun in the distance
This will be over soon

The cloud departs: a trailing ghost.

Loyalty card

IT STILL SEEMS to be a long time until I no longer require food, and here I am in the foyer of the supermarket, an empty wire trolley idling beneath my imperceptibly trembling fingers. The light is bright, and the smell is of nothing at all. My mind is blank. There is a route to be followed: straight ahead, turn right then right again, travelling aisle by aisle until (I am planning ahead) I end up in the wines, beers and spirits. My experience in these matters tells me that I will have run out of money by then, unless I am careful. I will have to be careful.

But almost immediately, things start to go wrong. Here I am, transfixed by the twitching red muscles in the meat aisle. This isn't very good. I take a deep breath and move away. Nothing to see here. There is the rattle of teeth, of fingernails, bones, in the cardboard cereal packets, sloshings of lumpy fluids in jars and tins, the muffled howls of the doomed. I jerk my head away from the cans of 'processed meats', the hanks of hair in the salad bags.

In the frozen food cabinets; plastic sacks of severed fingers, clingfilm stretched fetishistically over pale limbs, bent double and tied with white string, blood pooling darkly in the polystyrene trays.

Death warrants - signed, but with the name left blank - amongst the Sunday papers. The zone behind the translucent doors.

I can't do it. I can't shop. Looking determinedly straight ahead, I remove a bottle (whiskey? vodka? I am unsure) and stand in line at the checkout. Do I have a loyalty card? I stare in fear at my interrogator.

"Yes," I whimper. "I mean, no."

Lachrymose

MY LIFE WAS dust in a sunlit stairwell; tiny fragments of things that were no longer there, floating aimlessly, sinking slowly. I shared my room with a fly that moved erratically round the light-bulb. I copied its movements into a notepad, hoping that they would spell out letters, words, sentences. And that there might be some meaning there.

- on
- and on
- at
- last

Nothing, I thought. The fly lived in my room all summer and never said anything useful. Just round and round the lightbulb. Every day. It never seemed to rest, or eat. Maybe it slept when I slept. I didn't know much about that. It doesn't do to think too hard about sleep. Or love, or hunger. Some things get easier with thought, like mathematics. But other things are best left alone. Just going round and round.

I wanted to be like a piece of music played on a piano in a circular room at the top of a tower. When I looked out of the window I wanted to see a rolling pine forest stretching to the horizon. The truth was that my music sounded like traffic and my view was of a wall five metres distant.

Tear Wine.

4 1/2 litres (8 pints) tears

1kg (2 1/4 lb) white sugar

Juice of 2 lemons

General purpose yeast

Boil the tears as soon as possible after crying as they can very easily sour. Add the sugar to the boiling tears. Add the lemon juice. Start the yeast in a glass. Leave the tear mixture to cool to blood heat, then add the started yeast. Leave to ferment in a darkened room for three days then strain off into a 4.5 litre (1 gallon) jar and seal with an airlock. Bottle, cork and store when fermentation ceases. This wine may be drunk after a month but it is even better after six months.

- on - and on

- at

- last

No more parties

I WAS INVITED to a party held in the grounds of my fiancé's university. We were circulating in the grounds surrounding her department as the sky darkened and champagne was distributed. The first puncture of our lazy expectation was a brightly-lit container spinning across the night sky. It disappeared, then reappeared, drew closer and plummeted towards the arboretum at the front of the university. A spaceship the size of an articulated lorry plunged into the pines, which creaked and snapped as the ship drove into the earth. Two more tall pines fell as a wall of flame erupted into the black air, illuminating the university and the faces of the lecturers and post-graduates, who stared, slack-jawed, at the flailing, burning bodies of the Aliens as they attempted to disembark from the doomed craft. I couldn't tell if the Aliens wanted to join us. Maybe they wanted to invade Earth. It wasn't in the script. But even so, I couldn't tell if I felt good or bad. I think they buried the Aliens, but I don't know if anyone prayed for them.

Sky Sports

ONE DAY I found out that my urine was acting like a powerful foaming agent. I thought that I could take advantage of my ability by hosting piss-scented foam parties in the pub toilets, but the landlord wasn't keen. He didn't think that people would be interested. In fact, he said that it was a disgusting idea. I said I'd rather go to a piss foam party than watch the fucking football, but he said that I'm in a very small minority and the big screen stays.

Faded notice

NOTHING MUCH GREW around the village any more, except yellow nettles, giant hogweed, and twitch grass that strangled the weaker plants before they could flower. Both of the shops had been closed for ages, with net curtains hung in the display windows barely concealing the dusty emptiness of the redundant shelves, the avalanche of unopened junk mail below the letter boxes, and the ghosts which left no footsteps on the dirty linoleum floors.

Faded typescript taped to the inside of the door of one shop explained the falling-off of trade, the lowered profit margins, the forlorn blame laid at the automatic doors of the out-of-town supermarket thirteen miles away. I read this notice many times, as if one day it would explain more. There was no such explanation on the door of our house, though perhaps there should have been.

Things had been going awry between us for some time. We had difficulty in understanding one another somehow; as if we spoke different languages and our interpreter had more lucrative work elsewhere. We moved around each other in something approximating silence, in a wan ballet that owed more to exclusion zones than elegance or grace.

Often it seemed as if we were the only inhabitants of the village. On my aimless perambulations I would see no-one at all. No dogs, no cats. I saw only birds; crows circling high overhead in the white sky, calling out in the air, laughing, or perhaps crying. Their nests were knotted cancers high in the tallest trees. I watched them as they wrote indecipherable messages against the clouds. Not for me. No messages. I went home, and our front door was heavy as lead.

Along and then up

THE COUNTRYSIDE AROUND here was clearly built by malevolent children for acting out obscure and dangerous rituals. It makes me think of sharpness; the edges of broken glass and half-opened tins. Scissors. There's no-one around.

Litter scattered; blown on hedges and snagged on the thorns. The distant hedges look like marker pen drawn onto rough cardboard. There are straight lines of: Lombardy poplars, Leyland cypress, and ornamental cherry.

High-tensile security fences ring areas of blank land. I can see no reason for this. Perhaps something is going on but hidden, or about to go on. Something is going to happen. The land waits like a child waiting for a smack.

Trees are left alone in fields of wheat. Over there; destroyed electricity pylons, surrounded by orange plastic day-glo webbing. And I can see from here that there is Bad Weather at Heathrow. I am jittery and my hands are sweating. The aeroplanes pillowing up through the air look unrealistic.

I can see the planes taking off around the one I am sitting in.

The aeroplane people carefully perform

a disturbingly calm yet oddly theatrical safety demonstration.

Something out of a Laurel and Hardy film.

Clouds thicken and curdle like meringue over my head. The plane is going backwards. They keep saying "short flight". The lights are flickering, and it's raining.

FASTEN SEAT BELTS.

Taxiing for take-off. Wings changing. Runway ahead. I have done this before I have done this before I have seen Hounslow from the air before.

Lumbering over concrete runway slowly.

A grey sky and a sense of disbelief overhang this ridiculous field.

A brief booming of the engine like a growling gong. We stop again.

I consider the runway. It's pocked, painted and old-looking.

Speed.

Then a floating sensation that seems too slow. Toy houses and tiny cars. Lurching. The M4, is that? Clouds tilting. Nothing, white nothing. Lurching. White light, and into the sun above the clouds. So eerie and dead. The plane tilts and the clouds fall away. I can see peeling paint on the wing.

Blue sky.

A landscape of clouds, mountains, valleys, craters and seas.

I feel sick.

Everything is very white and blue. The plane is sort of steady. Looking down I imagine the cities and the people who I used to be certain lived in the clouds. I'm now above the cities I invented when I was on the swings at the park.

I shouldn't be here. I'm the destroyer of my own illusions, the death of my imagination, the bringer of all that is sensible and responsible.

If I had been strapped to the wing I would have been dead long ago; a frozen husk.

If I was to fall, how long would it take? What would the clouds be like?

The clouds are rippled like sand after the tide. They look like death will look, but I am suspended and safe from harm. If I fall the clouds will catch me. The shooting and explosions from my planet are silent, and the sky burns a harsh blue above the tilted wing of this floating abstraction..

There is nothing but blue and white, upon which this wing is pasted like a cut-out. I knew this couldn't be real. I always knew.

It's not here, that thing you're looking for

IT'S A DARK, grey, sulking day, and I'm in one of First Great Western's new train carriages. They are lit like operating theatres, the words 'emergency procedure' repeated on the back of every plastic seat. The sky is promising rain. I like the view from the window, even though I've travelled this way hundreds of times. I'm a commuter. And I like this time of year; November, melancholy days that never completely wake up, the trees scratching the sky with bony knuckles, the rivers in spate, the fields sated, a bilious green, more like fungus than grass. Pylon weather.

I'm very tired. Four hours of fractured dozing last night. I'm convinced that my eyes look weird in the reflection of the window, but it's hard to be sure. I can't stop seeing the landscape outside as it might be in the future; overgrown, smouldering, ruined, broken. Not Brave New World. Not even Airstrip One, more a shattered sprawl of wrecked retail parks, desolated industrial estates, a sky even more threatening than it is today.

I used to see a more traditional post-nuclear-apocalypse future, all snapped trees, rubble and silence. Now my future is more ambiguous – flood, desert, a polluted sameness. The future: like the present. Just the same. The future: an evicted squat.

Anyway. That's not what I wanted to write about. It's just hard to stop the mind from wandering when you're on the train. I'm going to be at London Paddington soon, and from there I'm going to walk to Fleet Street in as straight a line as I can easily manage, a line that goes due east. Here I go; London Street, Sussex Gardens, Radnor Place, Southwark Place, Hyde Park Crescent, Titchbourne Row, Connaught Street, Upper Berkeley Street, Portman Square, Fitzhardinge Street, Manchester Square, Hinde Street, Marylebone Lane, Oxford Street, Wardour Street, Saint Anne's Court, Dean Street, Bateman Street, Greek Street, Old Compton Street, Cambridge Circus, Earlham Street, Short's Gardens, Endell Street, Bow Street, Wellington Street, Aldwych, Strand, and Fleet Street.

It is an incantation silently mumbled by my slouching feet.

But there's no deluge; the sky has broken its earlier promise. Heathrow jets sparkle over the suburbs. A bright day in the canyons of London, an interrogative light cut into geometric fragments by the tall buildings. It's taken me an hour and a half to walk to Soho, with a stop in a Marylebone café on the way. I spend too much time with my thoughts. Too much time looking for spectres, phantasms, harbingers. I must get to Fleet Street before dark, otherwise I'll get nowhere.

Island of Doctor Moreau

I MARRIED DURING a sweaty fever of happiness and had been considering distaste for some years when it started. My face and chest began to feel too warm, as if I had run too far. On the morning following our third anniversary I awoke blearily, and padded to the bathroom where I found my mirrored self an impressionist caricature of what I expected. My skin had become my enemy; my self incarcerated within a prison that displayed my unhappiness publicly. I pulled at my features, pressed hard on my cheeks to bring a brief semblance of my previous normality to my face, but the details were all gone. I had to blur my eyes to see my past.

I left our house, and moved like a ghost through the streets, unhappily aware of the sharp three-dimensionality of my surroundings, the microscopic actuality of other people. I took short breaths, the air entering shallowly through my misty nostrils. It was like inhaling through cloth. I needed solitude, and walked quickly to the edge of the town. I passed along deserted roads, scuffing dust, keeping by the high walls in the shadows where I belonged.

It got late, and I worried that the dusk would assimilate me, that I would disperse like blood in the ocean. Reluctantly I returned home. My wife greeted me, and asked after my day. She talked for a while, but I didn't really hear what she said. I sat, morosely prodding at my face, unwilling to look at her eyes. I knew she would be squinting, making small head movements in an effort to force me into focus.

We divorced quite soon after. For a long time I thought that I understood why, but when I asked her one afternoon when we met in a cafe, she said I had got it wrong. It wasn't that, she said. It wasn't that at all.

My week

Sunday.

Turned on the telly. On BBC1 was "I'm So Lonely". On ITV was "You'll Never Be Famous". Thought of cranes, pylons, dams, volcanoes, locusts, lightning, helicopters, Hiroshima, show homes and ringroads.

Monday.

Read that for men under 34 the biggest killer is car accidents. Second is suicides. Spent a while wondering what third was. Hit my head against the wall a few times.

Tuesday.

Something without a name has been eating at my thoughts for a while. Standing in the checkout queue at the supermarket I feel violent, or bored, or hopeless, or depressed, or pointless, or just sick inside. Need only to see a headline of someone else's newspaper to feel frightened, or frustrated, or alienated, or helpless, or doomed, or just suicidal. Waking up was a battle with my limbs; stodgy, unreliable, wayward, hurting.

Wednesday.

Woke up. Found I'd forgotten how to tie my shoelaces. Basic cognitive functions then failed with increasing rapidity until all I could do was sit in a chair staring at the wall. Tried to phone for help but my arm wouldn't move. Eventually

Thursday.

Friday.

Saturday.

Romance

I WAS JUST staring out of the window, trying to see past my reflection on the rain-streaked black glass of the night train window. Then I heard a woman saying to a man "I thought you only drank one bottle of port and some champagne. Well, more fool me."

She sounded quite angry, but I didn't know the whole story and for all I knew she could have been completely justified in being angry. There was a kind of mumbling, then she said, "That's all very well. All very… clever."

I wondered what he had said that was clever. There was a bit more mumbling, and the next time the woman spoke she said "I don't want to go there. Simple as that." Straight away the man hissed at her "Simple as what? What exactly?"

I more or less glued my face to the window. "I mean, you haven't slept with me in weeks. Months," he hissed again. "Well," she said, "you don't want me to." The man hissed again, "It's not surprising. Your tone. It says it all."

We were the only people in the carriage, hurtling through the lightless wastes of England. Your tone. It says it all.

Idea

I HAD WHAT I thought was a good idea. I was thoroughly sick of myself; I was bored, angry and irritated with the person I had become. My early years had seemed quite promising, but when I realised exactly what that promise entailed, my enthusiasm for who I was died, as if introduced to a vacuum.

My idea was to reach down my throat with my fingers, grab hold of my insides, and pull them out of my mouth.

Quiet beckoning

IT IS AN old house that had once known grandeur but now has faded, motheaten curtains, cobwebbed windows whose sills are graveyards of dessicated insects, rising damp, mildewed furniture, dry rot, woodworm, subsidence, peeling wallpaper, rotten carpets, treacherous staircases, choking attics, dead smells, wasp nests, leaking ceilings, creaking doors, collapsed chimneys, grimy sinks, sagging floorboards, rat shit scattered corridors, cracked walls, crumbling plasterwork, dry toilet bowls, decades-old newspapers coated with decades-old dust on leaning tables, prone chairs, silent telephones, and vacant, forgotten ghosts who have nowhere else to go.

Though on the ground floor, in the west wing, is one single room where there is a small stove that burns gently through the day and the night. There is a comfortable chair here, threadbare on the arms. There is a narrow bed and a table that is clean. The floor is swept and the window, though small, is open on sunny days.

And if you want to come and see me, I will make you a cup of tea and try to remember.

Scent

I GOT INTO a fight in the perfume department
of a large store. It wasn't my fault; I had
been trying to choose a nice scent for my new
girlfriend and there was a scuffle to my left.
The perfume ladies backed away. I was filled,
at the time, with a sense of invulnerability that
came with having recently fallen in love, and I
stepped forward to quell the incipient violence.

Naturally I was punched, knocked over
and kicked in the face, but the broken bottles
of perfume released such an incredible bouquet
that I afterwards remembered the encounter
with a degree of fondness.

Telescope

THE GAP BETWEEN you and me. The gap between you and me. In art class, the teacher would say to look at the spaces between objects. That was how you could see what the objects really looked like. Well. Well, I was fairly certain of your shape. I'd looked at it quite a lot. It was the shape of billowing wheat or sad violin music or a quiet discussion in the coat-room at a party, or something. I wasn't so clear on my own. I had looked at it, in mirrors, or in confused reflections from shop windows, and to me it looked unremarkable. Just the shape of some man or other. Could've been anyone, really. When I tried to remember my shape it was the silhouette of a murderer, a torturer, a rapist, or some kind of fiend. There was no end to how bad my shape could be, when I tried to think about it. Our shapes, together? The gap between them was bigger every day. I couldn't see what we really looked like. The only thing I could think of was the sad violin music and the rapist; very far away, never any nearer.

Zombies

I WAS A bit stupid, not realising that zombies live amongst us. It wasn't obvious, and no-one had the fucking decency to tell me. So I wasn't blind; I was just ignorant. I mean, I had suspicions, feelings... whatever. Everyone has them.

The main thing about zombies, as I realised, is that they aren't very different from us. I've seen the films, and, well, they're not very accurate. Zombies aren't different from us at all. They don't eat people; that's just ridiculous. Unless they're desperate, I guess, and I've got to say: who wouldn't eat a human corpse if it really came to it? So that's the point. Zombies are just like us. You can't tell who's a zombie. So it doesn't matter anyway. Makes no difference.

Very cold

EVERYTHING WAS NORMAL and as it should be until one day I woke up and there was something wrong. I didn't know what it was, but it was a kind of persistent thing that I couldn't quite ignore. Something was cold and it was inside, not outside. It was like a place where someone had poked me with an icicle. A splinter of winter. The days passed like they do and I just got colder. The cold spread until I was like a sculpture of ice. I didn't sneeze any more, and I couldn't cry and if I tried to come it was like a tendril of porcelain. I was a solid man. You could throw rocks at me and it didn't hurt at all. I just splintered a little.

Perhaps fortunately, no-one noticed and everything carried on being normal and as it should be, all around me. But I was frozen.

Quilt

I AM THE noise that you hear at night. I am the lights you wish, in your heart, were an unidentified flying object.

Oh yes. It's me. It's not distant thunder and it's not a further distant atomic explosion.

It's me, in an aeroplane, bored nearly out of my mind.

And it's so beautiful up here.

I could walk to the end of the wing, and sit there, dangling my legs, looking down at the dawn clouds and the smeared reflected sunlight soaking the horizon. The circular engines are lit by a silver light. Everything is magical. It seems unreal, or impossible; and the clouds below – I can see them now. An endless, endless prairie of soft down, like the inside of an eternal quilt, like still foam on an unmoving ocean, layered invisibly upon itself, soft and safe.

We are flying slowly through blue soup. Tax my kerosene. Stop this idiocy.

Perhaps I'll fall asleep. My watch says 11:05. But whether AM or PM I don't know. Lost in a fog of timeless dullness. Oh, the romance of flight. Enough.

Attraction

I PUSHED THROUGH the crowd towards the main attraction. In a big glass tank was a naked man, standing there gazing ahead, not looking at us or anything at all. In the tank with him were millions upon millions of maggots, slowly chewing away at his flesh. As the writhing maggots gorged on the oblivious man, they visibly swelled and grew, and their sloughed skins were drawn along a glass chute by some kind of suction device into another glass tank where they rolled wispily together in their millions, glowing in the Californian sunset.

This was his act; standing in his glass cell, alive and fully conscious, he was stoically bearing his complete consumption by the squirming larvae that surrounded him. By sunset there would be nothing but a sinewy skeletal armature in the tank. And the crowds would leave, holding hands, moving easily into the dusk.

Camera

I TOOK SOME photographs in a dream. I took so many that I filled a 36-exposure roll of film. I took them to the developer's. They could develop them in 24 hours, 48 hours, or 3 days. I was quite excited about the photographs, so I decided to go for the 24 hour service.

When I got the photographs back I was disappointed, because they were all blank, just white rectangles. I thought that perhaps, if I stared at them for long enough, I might find myself back in the dream. I tried this for a while, sitting on a wet bench on a drizzly day in Regent's Park. It didn't work. A mother walked past with her child, who said, "the sky's not grey." But it was.

A green park for business

MEN IN PINK fluorescent coats are burying the dead by the side of the road. They are yawning. There is a solitary figure on the overpass, watching the traffic flow east. Three motionless horses are standing by some wet straw in the rain in a redundant field next to the business park which is all made of green glass held miraculously vertical in the brown mud.

That part is in development.

Next door is what I'd call a showcase. The immense green glass palaces are spaced perfectly amongst each other, and reflected cumuli flick gently across their surfaces. I like the trees; they are perfect, like the ones in architects' 3-D renderings. They have been planted in lines, wide avenues of hopeful saplings bordering new black tarmac car parks, freshly delineated into car-shaped boxes.

There aren't many people at work in these new premises, because it's Sunday. But the cars that belong to people who are either very keen or contractually obliged are parked very well, and at a certain distance from each other. The distance reminds me of the distance between men at a public urinal where there's room for them to be choosy.

I like it that these people are awake and working on a Sunday. I don't know, but it gives me a warm feeling. I'm envious of them. I imagine them in their cars going home along the A roads, or the motorway, and their cars will be warm with the radio playing, and they'll be thinking about, something. And they'll turn into the estate of new houses and their house will be in there and they'll know which one it is and they'll drive up and park and lock the car and get out and unlock the front door and everything will be all right.

I like it.

After the green park for business is a big housing estate that looks very new. The gardens have grass and white plastic garden furniture, often placed on patio areas. There are occasionally swings, but I don't see any children. It's quite hard to see much, because there is a high defensive rampart, ten or fifteen feet tall, running the length of the estate next to the motorway. On top of the rampart is a wooden fence to keep the noise of the traffic away.

After, I stopped looking.

Country walk

I HAVE NO idea how this happens. A nice lunch… there were, um, subjects discussed. A fond movement of heads towards each other. But despite my attempts at adulthood, there is a subtle calling from the woods in the valley. I open the french doors and tread alone across the wet grass while everyone watches the back of my head. When I at last turn I am sunk in shadow and the house is no longer visible.

Of course I carry on. I tread an old path that was so old that it's rusting. Flakes of rust settle on my shoes. Worn by many feet and more years the path delves into the red earth, and the first thing I see is a pigeon on the ground without a head. Plain and dead; on the floor with no head, only a bloody neck and a pigeon head that isn't there.

Of course I carry on. Next I see something else, a rabbit left lumpily on the grass with no head or legs in a gravy of blood, red against the wet green grass. Act brave, and nothing will happen. But I know: this isn't right.

So I enter the woods with rusty feet and my path is sunken and the day that I'd begun is a five-minute cartoon. Then the trees start to block out the light and the sun quickly seems almost a memory. Up there on a bank there's a man sitting and he terrifies me with his waving hands and silent white face. It is worse when I realise he has stumps instead of hands.

Of course I carry on. Next I see something worse, a huge tree and under the tree arranged as if for a photograph are a group of people staring at me. Most have no hands. Some have only one leg. Others have absent arms, and a few look as if they have sunk to their waists in the earth because of no legs. And they stare at me, each of them, slowly waving their stumps, trailing bandages through the air.

An almost atrophied sense tells me to turn around; to see a man of knives. He has too many knives. More knives than fingers, more knives than it is possible for a man to have. He has sharp knives of all sizes and he looks at me with no expression at all.

I realise that I will never leave this place, and step forward.

Practical jokes, again

NOT THIS TIME. Oh no. No way. I'm not fucking stupid.

I'm waking up and yes, everything's okay. Check the mirror. No Hitler moustache drawn in permanent marker on my upper lip. Good. Check my slippers. No mousetraps, no clingfilm bags of water, no drawing pins. This is getting to be tiring. Every fucking day; check, check, check. Where are my clothes? Still where I left them? Yes. Good. Unrumple every sleeve, inspect each pocket. Check. Okay. Get dressed.

Bathroom. Sniff the toothpaste. Examine my toothbrush. Toilet? Make sure there's no clingfilm stretched over the bowl. Have a shit. Unroll the toilet roll for at least ten sheets to check for insulting messages. Nothing. Okay. And now I'm going to have breakfast. It will take me a while to go through the cornflakes, so I elect to have toast and Marmite instead. It's possible there will be something in the Marmite, but I can't be fucked, to be honest.

Post! It's the postman. Or is it? Fucking hell. I just want to get on with my morning. Warily scout the hallway. Looks like three letters on the mat. Approach said letters with caution. Doesn't seem to be any cause for alarm. They're all for me. Two bills, one request for a charity donation which includes a free pen. Examine the pen. It's a normal biro. Head back to my breakfast, ensuring that the hair I left laid across the plate hasn't been disturbed.

The phone rings. Deep breaths. I've got caller display, but I don't recognise the number. Oh, right. I've seen the adverts; wind up your mate! Irate tax inspector! My daughter's pregnant! Oh yeah. Fucking bring it on. I answer. It's BT, wanting to know if I'm interested in broadband, and I'm not.

Fucking hell! I tell you, it's just exhausting. So I have a coffee, after making sure there isn't salt in the sugar bowl. That one, I tell you, is so passé. It's quiet now, and I luxuriate, lolling my head back over the chair and breathing deeply. Check my shoes, check my coat, and never, ever forget to check the pockets! Prime territory for all sorts of business, the pockets. Never forget.

The doorway in the hall is a likely spot too. Examine for tripwires, buckets, threads, and even these days those red laser pointers.

Right, I'm out. Should be okay at work.

Uneventful day. Looking forward to a rest though. Get home. Nothing's changed, nothing's changed. Stare at the phone. Go into the kitchen. Flip a knife this way and that way. Wish I had something to do. Wish I didn't live alone. Go to bed.

Some nuclear reactors

THE LATITUDE OF the Palo Verde nuclear reactor in Arizona is minus eighty-seven point one three one oh five. The longitude is thirty-four point three eight seven five oh. In California, the Diablo Canyon reactor is minus one hundred and twenty point eight five five four five, then thirty-five point two one one four two. In Florida, Turkey Point is minus eighty point three three one six eight by twenty-five point four three six oh four.

My own location is not so precise. I'm sitting in a chair and I'm staring at the wall.

Another fucking supermarket

As usual, I was in a supermarket. If I'd thought about it, which I suppose I did, there were quite a lot of places I'd rather have been. But... you know. I don't ever remember deciding to spend any time at all in supermarkets, but there I was. Trying to buy something. Something or other. I'd forgotten what it was, which pretty much seemed to be the supermarket's fault. There were a lot of aisles. A lot of light. I was amazed at the way people steered their shopping trolleys past those pushed by other people. That was just pure skill. When it was busy, people waited their turn for the baked beans, or, um, whatever.

Underneath the supermarket there were trenches where demons shovelled bodies – the dead, the half-dead, the wounded, the despised – into deep trenches. There was a horrible sense that everything was inevitable. Down there, things were dusty and left behind. They powered the lighting system with every regret the shoppers above had ever had. Even their subterranean sewerage systems were operated by regret.

Up above, in the supermarket, everything was keyed up for some sort of transcendental moment... the space, the light, the congregation. But nothing happened except for shopping. Um. No problem there, I suppose.

That would have been okay.

Really, it would. I could have coped, and everything.

Idiots

POSSIBLY I WAS watching TV.

But I'm not sure. There was some sort of war; the usual, really. The main thing seemed to be that people were shooting at other people. Not that anything seemed worth fighting about, but there they were, shooting and killing. Idiots. Anyway. Whatever. Bang bang, kill kill, dead dead. Nothing exciting. Nothing new. Anyway, I was watching this from some sort of viewpoint, and then I noticed something odd about the terrain. There were circular patches of ground, unnaturally green, unnaturally flat...

You're right. It was a golf course coated with war.

That's right.

A golf course.

I suppose that the camera panned round, but the strangest thing was what I saw next. There were some men shooting at some other men. A lot of them ended up being shot, and a lot of those men fell over. They were the dead ones, after it had all finished.

The strangest thing?

Yes, that was what I was going to tell you about.

Well, maybe it isn't so strange.

There was a man sitting on a folding chair, on one of the golf greens.

There he was, and there was a small folding table in font of him, with a glass on it.

His caddy was, with a shaking hand, pouring a drink into his glass.

And that man sat there, drinking his drink.

Maybe he was waiting for the war to be finished.

Daydream

I'M WALKING ALONG the lane, thinking vaguely that I am off to fetch the future from my unknown destination. Brown paper grocery sacks flip along the wet tarmac in the breeze, occasionally adhering to the ground where they slowly leak blood, again and again, to the sound of crows calling in a slow frenzy.

**Sell
your
house
and
buy
gold**

There was disaster coming; that was blindingly obvious. Life had been almost ridiculously easy, and now things were going to get worse. Much, much worse. I couldn't believe that I had ever thought otherwise. I couldn't believe that I'd ever thought that there could be any other outcome.

Listen to how stupid and idiotic my thoughts had been:

I had disregarded a thousand different types and variations of warning for years.

I had believed in the power of the authorities to deal with any situation that caused me foolish and irrational fears.

My bookshelves were full of learned books, packed with scientific explanations, and I had taken out a variety of insurance that implied my life was worth money.

Can you believe that? And here's more:

It was impossible to think that my life, or more precisely, the manner in which I lived it was effectively an inexorably lengthy suicide.

I did not much miss the butterflies, and birdsong had only reminded me of mobile phones or car alarms anyway.

Disaster I thought of in inverted commas; "DISASTER".

It was something that, if it were to happen, would look like extremely expensive special effects.

Because the world was big, and seemed to alter only in the details, I slowly became comfortable in many assumptions. I fossilised into what I saw as an eternally stable sediment.

In this state I engaged actively with property, clothing, money, culture, and had a vested interest in continuing to do so.

In this I was not alone.

Even though I had often observed newly-born swarms of mayflies smashed to pieces by a sudden and unexpected showers of hailstones, I often used credit cards.

Even though I myself had mercilessly crushed legions of ants beneath my feet, I took out a mortgage on a house that I then renovated, decorated and bought furniture for. And even though I had seen on the television many harbingers of disaster, I carried on acting as if nothing was wrong.

All of this was an error.

No. Not just an error; it was an immense mistake.

When, at last and unequivocally, I had to admit to my deeply comfortable self that disaster really was coming and that its coming was inevitable, I took certain steps.

Everyone that I knew of lived in houses, and it rapidly became clear that all of these houses were either too old, too dangerously situated, or in any number of other ways inappropriate. We used our diverse and highly-developed skills to research the question of what to do.

We decided to build a new house that had none of the drawbacks of previous habitats. We selected a site and had the house built. The disaster was definitely coming, but money still worked as it always had, as did credit, mortgages, property, and all the other things we clothed ourselves with.

The disaster was coming, but we found we still had time to build a house.

There seemed to be no particular urgency regarding the disaster; only a dull sort of inevitability. Our new house fulfilled all the requirements we sought, but there was one thing we had not thought about.

One thing we had not got right.

We built a house with too many shadows in it. It wasn't the sort of thing that you notice at first; oh no.

The shadows did not become evident until it was too late.

Of course. Not until it was much, much too late.

And soon it was clear to us all that the disaster was almost upon us. This we deduced from the undeniable fact that many of the things to which we had become accustomed began to stop functioning.

The telephones became unreliable, and there was often no money in the holes in the walls. There was no more petrol, which led to some very unpleasant scenes, both on the roads and elsewhere. People had certainly been guilty of selfishness before, but the stoppage of petrol made a lot of people act extremely selfishly.

In addition to our frequent and increasing daily troubles, the always awkward-to-reach call-centre employees whom we relied upon for many things were frequently completely absent, and when the telephone systems did actually work we were usually rebuffed by recorded voices that enticed us through several options before becoming silent.

One evening the television had nothing to show us.

And then, almost suddenly, it was no longer possible to buy newspapers, or indeed many sundries including soap, dish-washing tablets, razors, lightbulbs, vacuum-cleaner bags, or toilet paper, as the family who had owned the shop had gone. We tried to find other shops, but the families who owned them had gone too.

We now had to think about the how of getting, rather than the how much to get. This was a strain. It occurred to me, not infrequently, that our civilisation had, of late, begun to make the simplest things extremely tortuous. We had perfected what now seemed a psychotic level of complexity around simple human activities like eating, keeping clean, and moving from one place to another.

Our supply of electricity became erratic. At the end of a day filled with minor panics of one sort or another it was apparent that there was no more of it at all.

That was where our real problems started.

Looking back, I can see that they began long before that. Our problems began a long, long time ago, when they were invisible, and continued during their gradual appearance.

The problems grew and were nurtured by our casual indifference, our sneers, and the ignorant manner in which we chose to converse. Our gestating problems were the dark, inevitable spectre that accompanied us to the cashpoint, into work, to the supermarket, and into our gritty, tortured beds.

And after the end of the electricity, the shadows conspired against us.

The dark corners began to scare us more than the coming disaster. The disaster was imminent; that was clear from the disappearance of many things which we had assumed to be vital to our being. But the threat from the shifting shadows in our house was worse, far worse.

We began, almost imperceptibly, to panic.

However much we reassured ourselves that we were safe, that the disaster would flow over us, that we had stockpiled, that we were defended and guarded against every eventuality, the insistent shadows illuminated our vulnerability.

When night came, we fell to a brooding quietude, eyeing each other with suspicion, inventing justifications for our dark feelings.

We cloaked our hidden desires; we conspired with the shadows.

Nothing seemed to be happening.

The television, I realised, had been a sort of terminal that connected me to a wider understanding of events. And without newspapers it was impossible not to write my own internal headlines during my sleepless nights. Worry became constant; worry and enforced exile from everything I was accustomed to.

I had never envisaged a sort of loneliness that did not involve people. But in fact it was the lack of small items that I had previously taken for granted made me lonely. I missed tea, toothpaste, remote controls, coffee, ballpoint pens, margarine, AA batteries, and easy credit in high-street stores. I missed my favourite magazines.

And the dead silence that encloaked the telephone and the television made me lonely. And the hollow look in the eyes of the people – oh…

I could have been told this a million times; this will happen, this will happen, this will happen; and would I have taken any notice?

Of course I wouldn't.

And naturally, I would have been one of the first to complain about the slightest interruption to my own carefully safeguarded existence. Around and around I had wandered in my stupid world: idiot, idiot, idiot.

After the end of electricity, the nights lengthened.

We had to wait in the dark, listening.

Life had quickly become intolerable for some of us.

It wasn't that I found my existence more tolerable than theirs; only that I felt that I had a sort of fortitude, a sort of... wisdom.

Nobody was happy.

The light in the house became less and less;
the shadows, darker and darker.

Still we waited for the disaster.

And when I looked, when people moved in front of the windows in the grey light, their shadows cast quickly clattering dark talons across the floor. This only became worse as the light faded.

I forbade them from moving, as it had become impossible to tell shadow from shadow. Or shadow from human.

Mine was a necessary act, an act which intended to prove that we had to be strong and united against the looming disaster.

The man had always been unreliable, but certain events had proved to me that he was a liability. If it had not been me it would have been another who would have had to take that awful decision.

Nobody witnessed anything; not that it would have made any difference if they had.

I was not ashamed, and after a certain amount of uproar I explained my reasoning and my actions to the others. But I did not go into the details; if I had told them about his struggling, and how long it took, there would undoubtedly have been problems.

We carried his carcass beyond the perimeter wire and left it in a ditch.

Inevitably, there were people who objected, and they were next.

When disaster is coming it is difficult to see clearly, but somehow I could see through the shadows to the light.

A long period of unpleasantness followed.

As the people in the house became fewer the shadows seemed to increase in number and in density. Often I perused my fading bank statements, lost in a reverie of long-gone financial transactions. I disliked being disturbed. Yes. I disliked that.

The disaster was coming. That was clear.
There were shadows everywhere.

When I was at last alone, when the people were all gone, I waited for the disaster on my own.

On my own.

Last Days

IT'S ALMOST A year since I last undertook this journey. Late in the day, mist, bright noise and signs at the railway station that all wasn't well. "WHO CARES?" and "WHAT AM I DOING HERE?" Bold lettering in a font I didn't care for. I looked closer and realised quickly that they were adverts for God. Maybe God should change ad agencies, because these adverts just made me sadder than I was before.

The clouds and mist coagulate as I travel east. A possibility of clarity obscured. I was told that if there was no immediate danger I should await instructions. I was told that there was one way. Exit. One-sided business conversations on mobile phones and the quiet clatter of fingers dancing on laptop keyboards and dead trees and pylons and cars streaming past on the motorway and industrial sheds and dual carriageways and a sort of geometry of fascism. Bone fragments and plausible deniability. "I'm on a train", and this, the best one: "What we should do is move all the money!"

A businessman chewing gum, the tendons in his face twitching. Sainsbury's. Tesco.

"I'm on a train." Car park. Trading estate. Van hire. Self storage. The Union Jack whipping in the cold air. Who cares? What am I doing here?

Inflatable black rubber
stately home

I REMEMBER WITH an occluded clarity our inflatable black rubber stately home.

Back in those days we would wander the corridors in a kind of suspended conversation, words drifting like sunlit dust between us as we stepped forward, never knowing. Our feet would crunch the decades of dead insects that had ended against the grimed glass. The sunlight was millimetres away, but unknowable. You looked blankly from the high window and there was not much to see that I could see but probably many decodings for you. The black rubber radiated a claustrophobic warmth but I was cold to my bones and I wished I had a thicker sweater to keep away the shivers. Out behind the window some birds moved through the grey air writing words.

Behind us our past was filled with people and events, talk and activity, engagement and civility. It dragged us upstairs like a ghost. The floors bounced with a forgotten alacrity and there was a joy written there on the walls but all it said to me was 'get out, get out'. I couldn't remember the way out, or even if I knew the way in. I was carrying the jars of our dried shared life in a crappy old supermarket bag digging into my wrists and it hurt. I wanted at least a bus home but I was at home in our black rubber stately home. There was no bus and no home.

In the fuggy behind of my memory our past was flexible and allowable; there was a way to make an impression. Today when I try to make an impression I hurt my head against the wall.

Yesterday I asked if we could take our inflatable black rubber stately home out again; blow it up, and pretend that nothing had happened. But you said no: our tent would do. I cried my tears into another plastic bag and dropped it, unseen, into a bin.

A phone box

THE FEAR OF the dark and the fear of the dead and the fear of running towards the phone box on the hill. I went to talk to someone who might be able to help me with this. I was ready, I thought, ready to talk, ready to explain and to describe the ploughed field on the hill and the red telephone box that rang and rang and rang. Really, I was tired. So tired.

The room I was ushered into was calm and quiet, with books on the shelves and charts on the walls and an ambient lighting system.

And after I don't know how many hours, here I am. Waiting to hear what it is that I want to hear. Wanting to hear what I wait to hear. I love to hear it. It's a waterfall to a man who's dying of thirst. It's electricity to a man who's out of battery. It's an alternative to the ploughed field, and not having to answer the phone in the telephone box. That's what it's like. But I must tell you. I'm still tired. So tired.

Again. Again, I was running through the sticky claggy ploughed field, up the hill, and the phone is ringing.

Head and Shoulders

WHEN I MOVED to my new flat I was very happy but when I worked out that the whispering voices that I could hear when I put my head under the water in the bath belonged to dead people I wasn't happy any longer, particularly because I realised that every time I put my head under the water when I had a bath the voices were slightly louder than the time before.

I tried not putting my head under the water when I had a bath but every fucking time curiosity got the better of me and I had to try it just for a second just to check and of course, even half a second of that sort of thing would bother anyone.

I kept asking the landlord to put a shower in but he prevaricated and said things like what do you want a shower for thats a lovely old bath thats an antique that is look at it it's Victorian you'd pay top dollar for one of those at the reclamation yard.

It's all right for him. He hasn't got fucking dead people talking to him every time he washes his hair.

Here be dragons

I WAS SOMEWHERE south of somewhere, north of somewhere else, east of everywhere and west of nowhere at all. I had been wandering for days, along endlessly straight roads and tracks. My wanderings took me across endless, peroxide-bright prairies of barley which the persistent wind lashed into yellow oceans on which long, low black ships sailed with their unseen slave cargo of caged poultry.

I was here by mistake, I now knew. I had begun with the idea that my world, encircled and delineated by diaries, deadlines, telephones, newspapers, email, bank statements, bills, invoices, tax demands, mortgage payments; detail and description of ever complicating varieties, might be a creation merely of my own. Perhaps simply by removing myself from this apparently scripted existence I could discover an unknown species of reality that had been previously invisible to my blinkered senses.

In some ways I wished myself in an era when the known had faded at the edges, where civilisation petered out into blank spaces occupied with the superstition of the unknown; here be dragons. But England had long been charted in exhaustive detail by Ordnance Survey maps; maps which showed every building, each gradient, each brook and pond, every pylon. Useful, doubtlessly, but also somehow terrifying.

And what happened was this; browsing the Ordnance Survey section in a bookshop one morning, I had been first annoyed then intrigued by the absence of a certain sheet number. I crossed town to another bookshop. It wasn't there, either. To be certain, I checked at the library, where it was also absent. I began to be excited. More than anything, I wanted to be off the map. I imagined the roads becoming tracklike, sketched roughly over the terrain like tangled spider silk. I saw trees larger, hedges wilder, the shapes of distant mountains torn against a perfect sky. Above all I saw no people, no animals, and no birds.

I studied the map of the area just to the south of the empty zone where I determined to stake my nebulous claim. By train, bus, and walking I took myself to the top of this sheet. There was no road north, just a brambled gap in the hedge. I pushed through the clinging stems and looked north with a broad smile. I had told no-one where I was going.

I walked for a long time.

Later, much later, I began seriously to worry if I was anywhere at all. I had no idea when I would reach somewhere with a railway station, or a bus station, or a bus stop, or a minicab office. It became so quiet I hoped for a jet to split the mocking sky. That evening I travelled into what seemed a kinder landscape; the lanes suddenly began to meander and sink between hedges as the sun sank lower and the air cooled.

My rucksack was heavy and painful on my shoulders, and it was clear that I would soon have to find somewhere to put up my tent. At the brow of a gentle decline I saw ahead of me a dark wood massing about a mile distant. It was there I would spend the night. The wood began at a fork in the lane where a small cottage lay beneath the purpling shade of the twilit trees. At the gate stood a man, bent with age, holding a scythe upright, the blade swinging idly above his head.

He looked straight ahead. I walked on, into the chilly shadows of the trees which grew along one side of the lane. I walked until I was out of view before I lurched off the road into the wood. I squeezed through the shrubbish undergrowth, picked my way through a head-high tangle of brambles, and found myself alone in the wood. It was the most silent wood I had ever been in. It gave the impression of being dead, despite the foliant appearance it had given from outside. The dense leaves of the wood had been forced skywards by the burgeoning deadness of its interior. The expired leaves and twigs beneath my feet cracked like chicken bones. There were no birds. There was nothing here.

I'd made some kind of mistake. I was here, by mistake. I knew this with a certainty that was shattering. But night was irreversible, my situation was irreversible. I could do nothing except unpack my tent, erect it, and crawl inside. I couldn't do anything except that. I couldn't sleep, I couldn't think of anything except a distant, faded sound of a stone sharpening a blade. I heard or I thought I heard chicken bones snapping and a rusty gate that creaked painfully on its decrepit hinges. I lay in my sleeping bag with my clothes on, with my shoes on, staring straight ahead, defencelessly conscious of the sound of my breath, horribly awake, off the map and out of sight and away from the map.

Silently I begged for the dawn. Trees, skeletal in their naked brittleness, swept down, brushing the fragile canvas of my tent. There was some grotesque sort of distant footfall or anyway a noise I couldn't account for. And occasionally but always, the slow, sly, shrill cry of the gate, opening and closing impossibly in the cloaking darkness of the dead of the night. Maybe a sound formed itself into the shape of my name, twisted itself and warped its voice into a terrifying parody of my name and of my ideas and of my plans and of my future. Maybe a sound slithered into my tent shaped like footsteps or knife-sharpening or chasing or a hollow realisation of the impossibility of escape. Maybe that's where I still am, cocooned in a flimsy, fabricated defence against what it is that I desire most; a damned region that lies off the map, unpeopled, empty of birds, bereft of animals, where the sky is torn from the land, and where I am caught for ever, dessicating, last week's insect caught in forgotten, dusty spider silk, suspended across a corner of somewhere that will never be visited again.

Midsummer's Day in a graveyard

EASYJETS CRAWLED ACROSS the sky, into the west wind. I read; in loving memory of. And; what will survive of us is love, love is eternal, here rests for a time.

Perhaps the dead lie happily in the well-tended plots, or perhaps they prefer the forgotten, overgrown corners. Perhaps they prefer their names obliterated by time and the weather. Perhaps not.

There was only the sound of the strong west wind in that place, and I wasn't there for very long before I thought that I should leave.

Peace and quiet

ON A DARKENING winter evening I sought cover from the rain in a pub on either Fleet Street or High Holborn. I can't remember which. It had been raining incessantly, and I was wet, which was my own fault. I had left my umbrella at home and didn't want to buy a new one. I had spent the day walking around the back streets, unclear about what it was that I was looking for. I stood transfixed outside St John's Gate watching an aeroplane scratching the underside of the shredded clouds. Later, I came upon a dead market; a few hooded figures picking at the skeletons of the stalls, torn polythene struggling to escape with the wind as the rain pasted it to the tarmac. And I stood for some time at Ludgate Circus, staring at the yellow lines drawn as diamonds on the road, hypnotised by the endless passage of black tyres hissing through the rain across them. By this time the scant grey light that had accompanied me on my perambulations was fading, and I was extremely wet. I don't recall which direction I took, but as I say, I ducked into a pub somewhere nearby.

The place was quiet; a warren of rooms, it seemed to me. I peeled my raincoat from myself and eased my soaked hat off. I found a small table next to a gas fire that sputtered warmly below the red 'appliance condemned' sticker, and took out my notebook. I was part-way through what was becoming an interminable project that was frustrating me further with every turn that it took. I didn't know if any of these turns were the right ones, or if I was wasting my time.

My soaked clothes began to gently steam by the gas fire in the pub, though I felt cold, chilled deep to my core. I held a biro over my open notebook as I tried to make something useful of the small events of the day. The old walls of the building muffled the traffic's roar, and my thoughts seemed likewise faded. The yellow light from the tasselled shade reflected against the frosted glass in the window. It was a black night outside. The fire continued to wheeze and choke. I looked down at my notebook. 'There will be no Quiet. There will be no Peace.' My pen was poised above the final full-stop. I frowned, unable to remember writing the words. For the first time I gazed around the room. When I had come in I'd

thought the small room was empty, but now I
saw that a man was sitting at another table, his
back to me. He was wearing a cheap-looking
chalk-striped suit, with scuffed black patent
leather shoes. Leaning against the wall next
to him was an umbrella, water pooling darkly
where the ferrule rested on the floor. His
greying hair was slicked back from a balding
head, and the lines on his face continued
round the back of his neck. He was wearing
glasses. I realised I was staring, and looked
away. Sighing, I closed my notebook and
tucked my biro back in my pocket. I wondered
if it was still pouring outside. I gazed around
the room, seeing wood-panelling and a few
Victorian foxhunting prints. The man at the
other table had opened a briefcase that he
had in front of him on the table. From it he
pulled a sheaf of A4 papers, which had what
looked like monochrome photocopied passport
photographs on them, about nine to a page.
There were about four or five lines of what I
guessed were details about each person printed
under each photo. He shuffled quickly through
the papers, as if to count them, then started to
look methodically at each. His pen paused a
few times over certain of the pictures on each

page, but he evidently decided not to mark any of them. The light glinted in the portion of his glasses that I could see, and suddenly I had the uncomfortable feeling that he could see my reflection in them, and that he had noticed that I was looking at him. But he made no sign that he had. He continued to slowly leaf through his papers. Nevertheless, I looked away.

But I couldn't stare at the ceiling for ever, and I had no interest in the foxhunting prints. I found my eye was drawn back to that shabby man in that small, yellow-lit room. He had begun to spend longer on each page, bending towards the photocopied images, carefully reading whatever it was that was written beneath them. I had finished my drink, and gathered my wet things, about to leave, when I glanced once more at the man. He was closely studying an image on one of his papers. I now felt coldly certain that he had been aware of my scrutiny, and at that moment he turned his lined face towards me, studied me for a moment, nodded slowly and slightly, and mirthlessly smiled. He turned back before circling a photograph with his red pen.

I rushed past his icy presence, bolted from the room, along the passage and out into the cold rain of either High Holborn or Fleet Street. But not before I had recognised the face in the photograph, and read, unmistakably, my own name beneath it.

None of the above

LIKE EVERYONE ELSE, I fell into love to the soundtrack of famine and war. During this episode I failed to think much about it. I devoted my attention to the eyelashes and the freckles on her face. I was stung by a wasp, failed to recognise my face in the mirror, was the subject of laughter, ate little and infrequently, assumed I was unique, had difficulties with reality, crashed in my car, and lost my job.

Although none of the above were important to me at the time. I remember them only because I had fallen into love. Do you love me? I love you. Do you love me? I love you.

And nothing else mattered and nothing else happened. The famine and the war were like wallpaper.

If we had been murdered in our beds. If we had been forcibly separated. If our families had been killed. If we had lost our minds. If she had been killed. If I had been killed. If we had been beaten raped tortured stabbed shot tied up with barbed wire dragged along the road behind the tanks

None of the above.

None of that has happened to us yet.

East Croydon

FIRST; WET, BLACK rock. Blue plastic flapping fitfully. There must be a wind. Floodlights on tall posts, or maybe security cameras. Huge plastic sacks full of trash. So much trash. Museums of it. Graffitti painted over in a colour approximating bare concrete.

Below are roads, then a roundabout. A big sign says, courage, in capital letters. Everything has a coating of limp soggy brown dead leaves. The cars look balletic on the wet tarmac.

Torn scraps of blue sky. Black. Dark. Yellow light.

Obsolete brick sheds with blank windows and extinct chimneys, men in high-visibility vests, housing estates, blackened hedges, lumped fields, sagging parkland, empty barns, ragged fallow, serried conifers, saturated mud, burst banks.

Trees standing staring.

Then; acres of wet, empty rails. Another sign says, the snooty fox, in italics. Pylons. Pyramids of gravel. Industrial units, portaloos. Mud. Rubble.

Self-storage. I'd like to store my self. Not needed at present. Will call back later.

An empty football pitch. Studded boots sliding through mud, dog shit. Kwik Fit Waitrose. Industrial estate. Mobile homes immobile. And a portakabin remote in a field of trash. A distant mental hospital. Stockbroker homes.

A huge wet field. One man standing in it. Arms raised wide to the sky. The sun finally comes out. We will shortly be arriving in East Croydon.

Happiness: a guide

NO-ONE IS HAPPY and if they say they are they're fucking lying. And I should know; I've tried it. I've collected all the ingredients of happiness and rubbed the resulting mixture all over myself.

Not many people have done it. It's extremely difficult to get any of the ingredients in the first place, let alone all of them. Mixing them properly is also very challenging; a lot of people get it totally wrong by concentrating on one ingredient at the expense of another; an easy mistake to make. What you have to do is lie in wait for each, be patient whilst they congregate (which doesn't often happen) and then saunter over, introduce yourself, and invite them back to your place. Metaphorically speaking, of course.

But it doesn't end there. It's not simply a matter of assembly; you've got to add various sorts of seasoning if the whole thing isn't going to end up like some nauseating religious marzipan. What you want is an easily absorbed lotion that won't bring you out in a rash or make you smell.

Beware of commercial preparations, expensive luxuries, evangelical tautologies, meretricious platitudes and printed hyperbole. Anything that promises fast results or painfree acquisition should be avoided. Real happiness is, as I've said, incredibly hard to attain, requiring years of struggle, hurt, anguish, self-doubt, paranoia and lengthy periods of agonising melancholy. Anyone who tells you different is either fooling you or themselves.

Personally speaking, I have overcome these many obstacles. And you can too, if you're willing to work at it; but to be brutally honest, it's not worth it.

present within one month

6 67 353 170

pay MR O WILKINSON

72-00-00

amount not over ONE HUNDRED AND TWELVE POUNDS
AT 014-504 PO
NB766895D

hundreds	tens	units
==ONE	==ONE	==ONE 30

Date 15 FEB 2005

£ **111-30**

PAY 4457
OFFICE 1192
STAMP 526 ****

not negotiable

JSA   02FEB05-15FEB05

C
0137501

03-681 44571192   94231
MR O WILKINSON
66B HOTEL GARDENS
AMERSHAM
HP7 5BW

Alliance & Leicester
Commercial Bank plc
Bootle, Merseyside,
GIR 0AA

read carefully the notes overleaf   do not write or stamp in the space below   6673531707

SF52 9650 009399 08/04

⑈13750⑈ 72⑈0626⑈ 0699222 6⑈

6673531707

My Giro

I WAS IN a dreadful situation. The Department had got me. Usually I had been able to avoid these situations by earnestly prevaricating, feigning excitement at a new 'project' that I was certain would lead me to a paradise in which my Giro would be nothing but a faint memory. Never before had they tricked me into actually accepting a position of work.

Looking back, I should have known it. The man smiled at me, allowing no ambiguity about the way the corners of his eyes crinkled. I was ready for the usual questions, but I hesitated when he asked me if he was right in thinking I was an artist. I made an almost silent flopping noise with my tongue as he went on to tell me that he had 'just the thing' for me.

I had the horrible sensation that I was taking part in the tortured dream of some sort of prisoner. I felt a morbid chill low in my insides.

The man was almost gleeful as he opened a file and passed a piece of A4 paper into my hand. I listened to him saying something, but his words had no meaning. He may as well have been speaking Latin. I looked at the piece of paper. I was led to a small room. Somehow there was a biro, and somehow I was sitting down signing the piece of A4 paper, and my mind seemed very far away, and I listened to the crackle and fizz of the static that erupted from the carpet.

And suddenly I was walking down the concrete steps to the street and I was employed. I had a job.

The job was in a shop in a surprisingly smart part of the town. There were people, employed people, everywhere, all looking as if they needed to be somewhere other than where they were at that instant, apart from those who sat in the many restaurants that lined the streets. They looked as if they had been born to dine in precisely those restaurants. A wave of nausea coursed through me.

I sat on a bench between two saplings, and stared at the dust between my feet. I sank my face into my hands and began to moan quietly.

What was I going to do? I had to take the job. If I didn't take the job, or if I got the sack, or if I left, I was fucked. The Department wouldn't give me any more money. I either had to be made redundant, in which case the Department would reluctantly pay me my fortnightly allowance, or I had to become some sort of criminal, a life for which I lacked many fundamental skills. I had to take the job. I had no choice.

After some time had passed, I got up and walked to the shop and introduced myself, mentioned the Department, and handed over the piece of A4 paper. I made my mouth move into some approximate smiles, and expressed a dull sort of keenness. My keenness was, however, overshadowed by the enthusiasm of the two managers of the shop. They explained excitedly that the franchise was an entirely new concept in tattoo parlours, in that the tattoos already existed and were grafted onto the recipient. The tattoos were carefully sliced from the bodies of corpses, young corpses being preferable as the artwork would not have blurred and turned blue.

The corpses were stored in a refrigerated chamber at the back of the shop, where they lay stiffly, awaiting a wealthy customer who would take their illustrated skin for their own.

I thought back to the morning, when I had awoken at 10.30 and ambled across the town to sign on at the Department.

That life now seemed distant.

My tasks at the shop were not onerous, but I desperately missed my indolence. I was required to be at work early in the morning, when the streets were filled with strange smells and sounds I was unaccustomed to. At the shop I sat behind a desk and, when a customer entered, would talk vaguely with them, correlating their personal details with entries in a database. I saw the managers in the morning and at closing time, and at lunchtime they would leave the premises to dine in one of the restaurants.

I was not so lucky. The interruption of my routine had unbalanced my eating habits severely. A gnawing, acidic hunger plagued my belly, but the idea of eating my hastily prepared packed lunches was completely repellent. Consequently I began to focus unhealthily on what I imagined took place in the back rooms when the managers were working on the customers. During slack periods I would stare with unfocussed eyes at the computer monitor, images of scalpels and the dark blood on green latex gloves washing against the shores of my mind. I also thought often of Giros I had cashed in the past, each one like a beautiful girlfriend who had been everything I wanted, but whom

I had never really appreciated. I hadn't much cared for the Department, but from my chair behind my desk, behind the plate glass which glazed the shop, my memories grew fonder.

The idea of the tattoo grafts disgusted me. There was no art needed here. Despite what had been said to me, this was definitely not just the thing for me. I wanted desperately to be made redundant.

After several weeks the managers asked me if I would like a promotion. The franchise was going well, and one of the managers was going to open a shop in the next town. They were going to hire a new receptionist, and offered me a position on the team.

Darkly, in a gloomy corner of my being I clutched at my Giro, but it was further out of my reach than ever. Somehow, a piece of A4 paper and a biro had altered my life profoundly. I had no idea how to undo the alteration.

It was growing dark outside, and I was led into a room that was artificially lit.

There was much to learn, and at first it didn't seem possible that I would ever be on 'the team'. But the manager who had remained at the shop persevered, and eventually his sometimes manic enthusiasm paid off.

An effect of the arrangement that I had not considered was my increased wage. Startled, I moved to a nicer flat, and began to take an interest in shop window displays. At lunchtime I went to restaurants with the manager who had remained at the shop and I developed an interest in dining that was wholly new to me. It was only occasionally now that I felt hunger, and those times were like a dimly-felt nostalgia. I bought a bicycle, and at weekends I cycled out of the town to hills in the countryside where I would grunt and sweat my way to a summit, and there survey the land spread before me. Birds sang strange tunes in the trees, and the clouds formed distant plateaux.

The corpses never stayed on the premises for longer than was necessary. I surprised myself daily with the corpses. I learned how to push down gently with a scalpel until the skin gently popped and I was able to slice through the skin, bisecting freckles, drawing a straight line that curved acutely as I changed direction. Once the tattoo was encircled I lifted one edge and attached the clamps. The patch of illustrated epidermis came away relatively easily, needing few nicks and cuts at subcutaneous matter with the scalpel.

I developed a taste for Italian food, and gradually became known as a high-tipping regular at one of the restaurants. My favourite table, by the window, was always made available for me.

The summer drew on, and a thick, sultry heat settled on the town. I no longer used my bicycle since I found that I was arriving at work with dark circles of sweat under the arms of my shirts, which quickly grew uncomfortable in the air-conditioned office. I bought a car after learning to drive one. I found learning difficult, as there were three distinct pedals, a steering wheel, a gearstick, several mirrors, windscreen wipers, indicators, different sorts of lights and a complex dashboard featuring more dials than I could hope to decipher. And of course, there was a windscreen, the view from which required constant monitoring. However, I eventually overcame these difficulties, and was able to drive to work in the same state of forgetful bewilderment I was sure I shared with my fellow commuters.

I still sometimes thought about my Giro, but the numbers printed in the little rectangle on the right were indistinct and smudged, and I could not quite make out the amount.

After all, I had been able to mostly forget some of my girlfriends.

When I had been at the shop for about a year I was in the novel position of Manager. I had both a professional, and to a lesser extent a personal authority over two key workers who I referred to as 'my team', and two receptionists, one of whom also worked as my secretary.

In the morning I would look through the photographs of tattoos that had been emailed to me, choosing those which I considered would be quickly resold, or that were particularly artistic and would fetch higher premiums. Most of the surgery (or 'hackwork', as we in the team referred privately to it) was now undertaken by my colleagues, but I still preferred to handle particularly large or prestigious pieces.

After choosing that day's purchases and authorising money transfers, I tended to spend an hour or so with my money, moving it from one place to another, in a manner which resembled a ghost playing Patience. I had never seen my money, but I was reassured by the sequences of digits on my computer screen and drew pleasure from watching them increase.

At lunchtime I would walk to my usual restaurant. I had tried almost everything that had ever been on the menu, but my favourite remained spaghetti bolognese, and my white napkin caught splatters of salsa di pomodori as I ate.

The afternoons were largely occupied with administrative matters. I was now comfortable with A4 paper, but as biros still nagged at a haunted attic of my mind I preferred to use my computer and printing machine, signing letters with a fountain pen.

Quite often I would spend the evening with the receptionist who also worked as my secretary. We had sex in my new flat, where she would attach me to my bed with ties and belts before taking my erect penis into various parts of herself.

For a few frightened moments after my orgasm had subsided I worried that she would refuse to untie me, and I would be found by archæologists of the future on the rusting iron springs of my bed, my flesh mummified on my emaciated frame.

I now regularly bought newspapers, and felt comforted by the vast prairies of knowledge that I had assimilated. Often I would dispute political matters in restaurants and at the dinner parties I attended. Frequently I found myself with words falling from my mouth that I barely recognised, but as they met with approval or enthusiasm I did not worry much.

At night, when I was not fucking my secretary, I would spend many hours in the passenger seat of my car, looking out of the window at the interior of my garage, which shimmered in my eyes, my bicycle shadowed on the bricks, interrogated by the fluorescent striplight.

More time passed, and I was being paid considerably more money whilst actually having less to do. I now often visited other people's offices, and they often visited mine. I became adept at handling biros, A4 paper, and the use of argument and persuasion. I was pleased that many meetings proved successful if held in restaurants, particularly if we all got drunk. I decided to extend the franchise overseas, and asked my people to arrange it. This happened easily, without my having to alter my habits very much. I found air travel less harrowing than I had first imagined, as I had a propensity for queuing.

Deluges of A4 paper were used in a deft manouvering of intangible properties, and the numbers I surveyed on my computer screen grew laterally. I was now rich, and wondered what my face would look like in photographs.

And then my life fell into small pieces. The letter from the Department was delivered, after being redirected four times, to my new offices. I was choosing the paint, but the subtleties of green were forgotten when I recognised the logo on the envelope. I requested that the interior designer should go away by making a gesture I had copied from television. With shaking fingers I opened the envelope and pulled from it a piece of A4 paper, folded twice.

It generically congratulated me on my new job, and had a computer-printed signature. There was also a questionnaire to fill in. Was I happy in my new employment?

I dropped the piece of paper, and stood in my new office, a wealthy and successful man. A wind of immense sadness billowed the corners of my mind, my Giro fluttering forever out of my reach.

I walked a little way and sat down on a bench between two saplings, and stared at the dust between my feet. I sank my face into my hands and began to moan quietly.